DENNIS the MENACE

THE MAGNIFICENT MENACE!

BEANObooks

published under licence by

meadowside
CHILDREN'S BOOKS

COWBOY CHAOS

It was the most dreaded time of the year. Some people were boarding up their houses and going away for six weeks. Some people were building extra defence around their homes. It was the summer holidays in Beanotown, and that meant just one thing. Dennis was on the loose.

"WHEEEEE!" Dennis cried as he shot through Beanotown on his skateboard.

"ARRGGHHHH!" screamed the postman as Dennis used him as a ramp.

"GNNNAAASSHHH!" barked Gnasher as he tore off a piece of the postman's trouser leg.

Dennis screeched to a halt on the other side of town and grinned down at Gnasher. "An excellent morning's work, my menacing mutt!" he chortled. "Did you see the look on Sergeant Slipper's face when he saw his underpants on the flag pole?"

Gnasher sniggered and Dennis looked up at the building beside them.

"Hey, I've never seen this place before!" he said. "It must be new! Awesome – brand new people to menace!"

It was a tall house, painted a violent shade of pink. There were lace curtains in all the windows and a big yellow bow on the front door. A sign outside said:

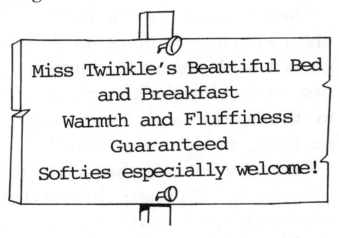

Miss Twinkle's Beautiful Bed and Breakfast
Warmth and Fluffiness Guaranteed
Softies especially welcome!

"Oho," Dennis chuckled, rubbing his hands together. "Brilliant! Miss Twinkle is gonna see stars!"

Just then one of the windows flew open and Dennis heard a loud voice.

"If you think I'm gonna sleep under a FLOWERY BLANKET, you're MENTAL!"

"Do as you're told, my lad!" yelled a man's voice. "We've come here for a peaceful, relaxing holiday, and that's what we're going to have!"

"Just because you've hidden all my menacing equipment, doesn't mean I can't menace!" shouted the first voice. "I'm the greatest menace in the world, and I can menace anything, anytime, anywhere!"

Dennis's eyebrows shot to the top of his head. "Oh yeah?" he growled. "We'll see about that!"

"One more menace from you, and I'll lock you up in this room for the rest of the holiday!" bellowed the man.

"You can't lock me up in a flowery, softy room like this!"

Something zoomed out of the open window and landed at Dennis's feet. He looked down at it. It was a toilet-roll cover in the shape of a princess, wearing a knitted pink dress. Dennis and Gnasher took a couple of steps away from it.

"I would've chucked it out of the window too," Dennis admitted. "But that doesn't change anything. I'M the greatest menace in this town, in this country and in the whole world, and that kid needs to know it!"

Just then, the door of the guesthouse opened to reveal a boy in a cowboy costume, with his hands on his hips. The boy pushed his Stetson to the back of his head and scowled at Dennis.

"Who are you?"

"That's my question," said Dennis, scowling back at him. "This is my town, and you're on my menacing patch!"

"Now it's MY menacing patch," said the boy. "I'm the greatest menace in the world! I'm here for a week, so you'd better stay outta my way if you know what's good for you!"

"You're making a big mistake," Dennis said darkly. "Beanotown ain't big enough for the both of us."

Dennis's hands moved slowly to the water pistol in his pocket. The guesthouse door creaked. A single paper bag blew down the street.

"Max!" bawled a voice from inside the guesthouse. "Get in here now!"

Max's eyes narrowed. "We'll finish this later," he said.

"Running in to mumsy?" said Dennis with a grin. "You're no threat to me, flower boy."

Max's hand flew to his catapult and he hurled a rotten tomato at Dennis's head. Dennis moved like lightning, using his catapult to fire an egg at Max, but Max ducked and it flew over his shoulder and hit a lady in the face. The egg dripped down over her top.

"EEEK!" she squealed. "Miss Twinkle, I presume," chortled Dennis as he scarpered.

Back in their den, Dennis and Gnasher sat snaffling a plate of sausages.

"There's no way that cowboy's gonna get away with calling himself the best menace in the world!" Dennis growled.

"GRRNNNAASSHH!" Gnasher agreed.

"This calls for something special," said Dennis.

He pulled out his box of top menacing equipment. He ran his hands over boxes of super-strong stink pellets, trays of extra-loud whoopee cushions and packets of dried insects. He picked up his two best water pistols and weighed them in his hands. "We'll see who gets to menace this town, once and for all," he said. He filled his water pistols with ink, oiled his catapult and stuffed his largest water bombs into his pockets. "Time to show Max how wrong he is!"

Beanotown will never forget that day!

Shops closed early, softies ran for cover and traffic came to a standstill as Dennis and Max rampaged through town.

Max laid a slippery oil trap for Dennis. Dennis rolled over it on his skateboard, did a giant flip and crashed through the Colonel's hedge,

knocking the garden gnomes for six.
Then he flipped again and came out
at the other side, slammed onto the
pavement and sped away.

"Curses!" snarled Max.

"You're not messing with an
amateur!" yelled Dennis.

"My garden gnomes!" sobbed the
Colonel.

Dennis set up a water-bomb ambush for Max, underneath the old bridge. Max spotted it at the last minute and fired his peashooter at the dangling water bombs, exploding them all over Walter the Softy's mumsy.

"My new hairdo!" cried Walter's mumsy.

"Bad luck!" cried Dennis, clapping his hand to his forehead.

"Yeehaw!" yelled Max, firing the last water bomb so it splashed down Walter's mumsy's neck.

They raced back into town. It was a busy day and the streets were filled with people, including Lady Deighton, who was wearing a brand-new outfit and had come in to town to show it off. Dennis drew his ink pistols and fired both barrels as he dived for cover behind Spotty Perkins, who was out shopping for a new bow tie. Over Spotty's terrified shoulder he fired jets of ink at Max, who shielded himself behind Lady Deighton.

"My new dress!" screamed Lady Deighton, as her white dress was splatted with huge dollops of black ink. "I look like a Dalmatian! What will I tell my husband?"

"Just say it's the latest fashion!" Max chortled, sending a volley of stink pellets over her shoulder at Dennis.

"Good block, Spotty!" grinned Dennis, as the stink pellets smashed into Spotty's chest and dripped down his blazer.

Dennis skidded into a turn and headed for the park, scattering a large group of geese as he sped past. When Max appeared in the park, Dennis hurled bits of dry bread from his pockets at him, and the geese went crazy! Max was hidden by a flurry of feathers! His catapult and peashooter went flying in different directions as the geese fought for the bread.

"Ho ho!" Dennis chuckled. "What kind of cowboy gets ambushed by geese?"

Suddenly a lasso came flying out from under the huddle of birds! It snagged Dennis's skateboard and took it flying through the air to Max's waiting hand. With a yell of "Hi Ho Silver!" he sent the geese flapping in all directions, and zoomed straight at Dennis.

"Not so fast!" grinned Dennis, grabbing a branch and hurling it at the skateboard. The branch jammed the wheels and Max somersaulted over Gnasher's head towards the pond.

"GNEE HEE HEE!" Gnasher laughed.

"Time for a swim!" Max bellowed. He clutched Dennis's collar as he flew past him and with a huge SPLASH! they both landed in the middle of the park pond.

"YUCK!" said Max, spitting a small fish out of his mouth.

"That was a pretty awesome move with the lasso," said Dennis, wiping pond water out of his eyes.

"Your ink pistols were a stroke of genius," Max admitted, grinning back at him.

Suddenly they heard a familiar bellow of rage. Sergeant Slipper was standing at the edge of the pond, next to the park warden.

"The Sheriff!" Max yelled in delight.

"Scaring the geese!" burbled the park warden. "Polluting the pond! Clap them in irons!"

"You come along out of there right now!" shouted Sergeant Slipper. "I'm going to have you both grounded for the rest of the summer holidays!"

"Grounded?" scoffed Max.

"There isn't a parent alive who could ground me!" Dennis declared.

"You two are going to be sorry!" Sergeant Slipper hollered.

"Would you like to bet on that?" Dennis asked with a smirk.

The two menaces exchanged glances.

"Are you thinkin' what I'm thinkin'?" said Dennis.

"Sure thing," Max drawled. "A Sheriff like that calls for a menacing truce!"

They shook hands and heaved each other up out of the water. Then their hands flew to their catapults. Sergeant Slipper and the park warden were caught in a hail of stink pellets and water bombs.

"ARGGHH! HELP!" they cried, trying to find cover. Dennis and Max advanced out of the water.

"I'm out of ammo!" Max yelled. "They're escaping!"

"Look around you!" Dennis chuckled. They picked up handfuls of soggy pond weed. Max catapulted a long piece of weed at Sergeant Slipper, sending him blundering into the bushes. Then Dennis fired a piece of weed at the park warden's bottom, and he went down like a bowling pin.

"STRIKE!" whooped Max. "Awesome shot, pardner!"

They raced away in the direction of town.

"That Sheriff needs to be taught a lesson!" Max panted as they charged along.

"I know just the thing," Dennis chortled. They didn't stop running until they reached the police station. Max looked at his watch. "That slowpoke Sheriff won't be back for ages," he said. "How's about a few improvements around the station?" "I like the way you think!" Dennis grinned, and they got to work.

Fifteen minutes later, Sergeant Slipper staggered back into his station. Pond weed dripped from his hat and his uniform was splattered with stink pellets.

"Just wait until I get my hands on those pains in the neck!" he seethed. "I'll give 'em pond weed!"

He pulled off his tunic and hat, and went to wash his face. At the window, Dennis and Max sniggered. They watched as Sergeant Slipper reached for the soap and lathered his face and neck. He splashed water on himself and then glanced in the mirror.

"YARRGGHH!" he cried. "I'M BLUE!"

"Blue-dye soap, the very best!" Dennis snorted.

"Now his face matches his uniform!" added Max with a burst of laughter.

Sergeant Slipper tried to scrub the dye off, but it was no good. He pulled on his spare tunic and did up the buttons. Then...

"YOWCH! EEK! OOH!" he yelled, dancing around the room and scratching himself like a chimp.

"Itching powder in the sleeves," whispered Max.

"Inspired," Dennis grinned.

28

"I'll write a report this instant!" Sergeant Slipper ranted. "I'll tell their parents everything!"

He picked up a pen and started to write, but it suddenly gave a loud POP! and black ink squirted him in the face. Outside, Dennis and Max were crying with laughter.

"Exploding pens, the latest brand!" Dennis snorted.

Sergeant Slipper reached into his desk for another pen and...

"OEARRRGHH!"

He danced around the room with a couple of squishy rotten tomatoes dangling from his fingers! Dennis patted Max on the back.

"It's an old 'un but a good 'un!" he grinned.

"That's it!" Sergeant Slipper howled. "I'll arrest them both! And that dog!"

"Quick!" Dennis ordered.

They dived into the bushes outside the station as Sergeant Slipper came marching down the path, his face blue, his ears red with rage and his fingers dripping tomato goo.

"Now!" Dennis hissed.

They flung two long, rubber snakes in front of Sergeant Slipper and wiggled them crazily.

"SNAKES!" screamed Sergeant Slipper. "ADDERS! PYTHONS! MUMMY!"

He turned tail, ran back into the station and slammed the door. They heard him bolting it at top speed.

"Excellent menacing!" Dennis hooted, falling backwards and holding onto his stomach as he laughed.

"Sheriffs are always cowards!" Max added.

"You know what," Dennis said thoughtfully, "we're both top menaces, but together..."

"Our menacing power is outta this world!" Max finished.

Two menacing grins spread over two menacing faces. Dennis rubbed his hands together gleefully.

"Beanotown, watch out!" he chortled. "This summer, you're gonna get double trouble!"

THE MYSTERY MENACE

"NOOOO!"

The noise was so loud that some of the houses in the street shook on their foundations. Pictures fell off walls. Lumps of plaster dropped from ceilings.

"THIS HAS GOTTA BE ILLEGAL!" Dennis bellowed, as the glass shivered in the window frames. "WHY SHOULD I HAVE TO LOOK AFTER SOME SOPPY, STUPID, GIRLY GIRL?"

"Because she's your cousin and it's your duty!" Mum yelled back at him. "Back me up, Dad!"

"I'm not getting involved," said Dad, shrinking behind his newspaper and slipping some earmuffs on.

"She'll be here any minute!" Mum went on. "You're going to be nice to her or I'll stop your pocket money for a YEAR!"

"You've ALREADY stopped my pocket money!" Dennis hollered.

"Then I'll stop your comics!" said Mum furiously. "Aha!"

"BLACKMAIL!" Dennis roared.

"Yes," said Mum simply. "Now you had better be nice and show her around Beanotown, or you'll be sorry!"

Dennis opened his mouth to argue, but just then the doorbell rang. He flumped down into a chair, folded his arms and glared straight ahead. Then Mum walked in with a girl who sent chills up and down Dennis's back.

She had smooth, black hair in two neat pigtails, a pink satin dress with a high, white-lace collar and a pair of dainty, high-heeled shoes with bows on them. Her white ankle socks were fringed with pink lace and her cardigan was soft and white and fluffy.

"She can't be my cousin," muttered Dennis in horror. "She can't be related to me!"

"It's lovely to have you here, Posy," said Mum.

"Thank you for having me, Auntie," said the pink apparition.

"Posy?" mumbled Dennis, shaking his head in disbelief. "Her name is Posy?"

"We'll put your bags in your room, and then Dennis can show you around Beanotown," said Mum. She glanced at Dennis over her shoulder. "One menace on Posy, and you'll never read a comic again!"

Dennis glanced out of the window, and saw Curly strolling past with his hands in his pockets. He dashed outside.

"You coming?" asked Curly. "I'm off to meet Pie Face. We're gonna booby trap a teddy bear and give it to Bertie Blenkinsop!"

"Sounds like fun," said Dennis, "but I've gotta give a guided tour to the pink peril."

He explained, and Curly gave a wide grin. "I guess that means that you won't be doing much menacing for the next few days?" he said. "That leaves things free for me!"

"You reckon you can menace as well as I can?" Dennis scoffed. "In your dreams!"

Curly tapped his nose. "I've got a few ideas up my sleeve," he said. "Just you wait and see. Maybe you're not the only top menace in this town!"

"Do I look worried?" Dennis grinned.

"See ya later," Curly said.

"As if Curly could out-menace the Menace!" Dennis chortled. "Yeah, right!"

He turned back to the house, and stopped.

"But even so," he added, "there's no harm in thinking up a few new menaces, just in case..."

The rest of the afternoon was a complete washout. Dennis walked all over Beanotown with Posy, and he didn't have chance to do a single menace. Gnasher came too, and got almost as depressed as his master.

"Oh look!" cried Posy, as they walked back through town. "A lovely flower shop! Oh, I would love to buy a bunch of flowers for your mummy, Dennis."

"How about some fake flowers from the joke shop?" Dennis suggested. "They've got some roses that squirt custard at whoever sniffs 'em!"

"That's a horrible idea," said Posy, staring at Dennis with disgust.

Dennis rolled his eyes and shrugged his shoulders.

"Go and buy the stupid flowers then," he said. "But don't expect me to come in with you. I got banned after I made the ceiling fall down a few months ago."

Posy gave him a nervous look and hurried into the shop.

"Maybe that's the answer, Gnasher!" said Dennis. "If I scare her with stories of menacing, maybe she'll go home early!"

"GNASSSHHH!" said Gnasher hopefully. Just then, there was a loud roar and the Colonel charged past them, with a lobster clinging to his bottom.

"This is your doing, you menace!" the Colonel yelled as he raced away. "A lobster on my bicycle seat, by jove!"

"So Curly's started already," chuckled Dennis. "Not a bad menace! But why stop at one lobster? Curly'll never be a top menace if he doesn't think big!"

"What was that noise?" asked Posy, coming out of the shop with the flowers. "Just an average day in Beanotown," Dennis chuckled. "Posy, let me tell you a little bit about menacing..."

When they got home, Posy gave the flowers to Mum and then raced upstairs and into her room.

"What have you been doing?" asked Mum suspiciously.

"Nothing!" Dennis promised. "Not a single menace. I've just been telling Posy a few things I've done around Beanotown…"

"No wonder she's upset!" said Mum. "Well, you're not going to do it any more! It's May Day tomorrow, and I think Posy would love to take part in the dancing. I've asked Walter to come over and teach her the steps."

"Excellent," Dennis grinned. "If she's skipping round a stupid maypole with softies galore, she's not bothering ME. Let's go, Gnasher!"

Dennis raced over to Curly's house, but he wasn't there.

"Hmm," said Dennis. "He must be out menacing."

He skateboarded towards town, but on the way he heard someone calling out to him from the pavement.

"Oy! Menace! You did this!"

Minnie was standing there, glowering and shaking her fists. Dennis stopped and stared at her.

"Just you wait!" she bawled. "When I get outta here, I'm gonna minx you good and proper!"

She was struggling to move her legs, but she wasn't going anywhere. Dennis hopped off his skateboard and strolled over to have a look. Minnie was standing in a patch of something black and sticky. Dennis sniffed it, and then a smile spread over his face.

"Extra-sticky treacle!" he declared. "I'd know that smell anywhere! Someone's been busy!"

"Not a bad idea," Dennis chuckled, walking off. "But he's still not up to my standard! I'd go for a dollop of treacle on every doorstep in the neighbourhood!"

As Dennis walked past the butcher's shop, the butcher banged on the window. His eyes were popping out of his head.

"I'm not sure I like the look of this…" said Dennis, checking out his escape route.

The butcher came pelting out of his shop.

"You young ruffian!" he shouted. "My assistant's no good to me like this!"

He pointed to the back of the shop, where his assistant was blundering around with a bucket on his head. Dennis exploded with laughter. He had a bone to pick with the big-eared assistant.

"Awesome menace!" he chortled. "Your assistant tried to kick Gnasher last week! That'll teach 'im!"

"That bucket'll never come off in a month of Sundays!" growled the butcher.

"Not with his ears," Dennis agreed, jumping onto his skateboard.

"Come back here!" fumed the butcher, as Dennis and Gnasher shot off down the street.

"I've gotta find Curly! That bucket menace was genius! I wanna know how he got that bucket on so tight!"

Dennis spent the whole afternoon hunting for Curly without catching a glimpse of him. But everywhere he went, voices called out at him.

"You nuisance!"

"You pest!"

"My little boy has elderberries in his hood!"

"My little girl has spiders in her vest!"

"My shed door is missing!"

"My dolly is bald!"

"DENNIS, YOU'RE A MENACE!"

Dennis sped past them all, waving his hand cheerfully and taking the occasional bow.

"This is totally awesome!" he told Gnasher. "Curly is working his socks off thinking up original menaces, and I'm getting all the credit! That's the biggest menace of all!"

When Dennis got home, Dad was just signing the last of several cheques for an angry queue of people at the front door. Dennis crept around the back and went into the kitchen. Mum was baking cakes with Posy.

"Oh, it's been a lovely day, Auntie!" gushed Posy. "I practised maypole dancing with that handsome boy Walter, and then he invited me to a doll's tea party with his friend Bertie."

"Handsome!" gasped Dennis, sticking his fingers down his throat. "Are you sure she's my cousin, Mum?"

"I want you to be on our best behaviour tomorrow," said Mum. "Posy will be representing the family. Oh, it's so wonderful to have a little girl who's interested in clothes and dancing! Bea's only interested in hitting people with her rattle!"

"Quite right," Dennis chortled.

"There's only one way to represent this family tomorrow," he added under his breath with a grin. "And that's with a bit of good, old-fashioned menacing!"

In the morning, Mum went off early with Posy to get ready for the May Day dance. Posy was wearing a hideous violet dress with a high ruffle around the neck, and her hair was ringletted. Dennis rolled his eyes and prepared his weapons.

SOPPY FORTUNES

IGE'S

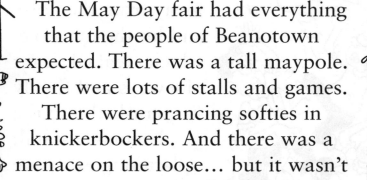

The May Day fair had everything that the people of Beanotown expected. There was a tall maypole. There were lots of stalls and games. There were prancing softies in knickerbockers. And there was a menace on the loose... but it wasn't Dennis!

While Dennis was getting into position in his hiding place, a mysterious figure in red and black was weaving in and out of the stalls, toppling toffee apples and shoving custard pies into faces. Dennis was about to hurl his first weapon (a water bomb filled with stink pellets) when he heard a yell. A red-and-black streak raced up behind the softies with an enormous balloon and a long pin... BANG!

"EEEK!" squealed the softies. They leapt away from the noise and hit the maypole, which creaked, leant sideways and finally crashed into the lemonade stand, splattering everyone with sugary pop!

"Curly is better than I thought!" said Dennis, when he had stopped snorting with laughter. "And faster... I've never seen 'im run like that!"

The red-and-black streak scooted past his hiding place, firing at the sobbing softies with a peashooter. Dennis frowned.

"Wearing my colours?" he said "He's gone too far! Time to teach 'im a lesson!"

He grabbed a rope, whirled it above his head and flung it far into the distance. The red-and-black figure gave a yell as the lasso grabbed him around the ankles.

53

"Heh heh!" Dennis sniggered, as he hauled the would-be menace towards him. "Time for a few just desserts!"

But as he pulled the figure closer and closer, Dennis started to frown.

"That's not Curly," he told Gnasher when he saw messy black hair. "And that's not just like my jumper – it is my jumper! I don't believe it... Posy!!!"

His cousin scrambled to her feet and pulled the lasso off her ankles.

Dennis threw back his head and laughed out loud. "So you've been doing all that fantastic menacing?"

Posy blushed. "Yeah," she admitted, scuffing the toes of her black boots. "I knew Auntie would never let me come and stay if she knew what I was really like!"

"So why did you want to come?" asked Dennis.

Posy grinned. "You're famous in the family! You're totally, like, inspiring!"

"I knew a cousin of mine couldn't really be so wet!" Dennis chuckled. "So you weren't really learning dance steps with that softy?"

"Nah! I was busy menacing Beanotown!" chortled Posy. "I just slipped away while Walter was talking about his teddies!"

"Right," said Dennis, pulling his catapult out. "Time to show me what you can do! Your gags are great – but some of 'em could do with a little work to become top menaces!"

"Lead the way!" Posy grinned. "I'm here to learn from the master!"

"I've got a feeling that your visit is gonna be fun after all!" chuckled Dennis.

WICKED WINTER

"Winter!" Dennis grinned, stomping out into the garden and making huge prints in the snow. "I love winter! It's the school holidays, it's snowing, and Mum and Dad are in bed with a cold. WICKED!"

He looked up and down the street. The wind was whipping the snow into strange shapes. A storm was brewing.

"Time for a bit of menacing action!" Dennis chuckled.

He jumped on his skateboard and slid down the street towards Curly's house. Walter the Softy was out in his garden with Spotty Perkins, building a snowman. They tried to hide behind each other when they saw Dennis.

"Aren't your dainty fingers getting cold?" Dennis chortled, leaning over the fence. "Go away, you menace," squeaked Walter. "We've got thermal gloves and vests and long johns," added Spotty.

"I don't wanna know!" Dennis snorted. "Your snowman's looking a bit lonely. Here, let me give you a hand!"

He picked up a handful of snow and threw it onto the roof. He watched as the snowball rolled back down, growing bigger and bigger. Then SPLAT! It landed right on top of Walter and Spotty.

"There, now your snowman's got some friends!" he grinned. "You can thank me later, I've gotta go!"

"MFFMMNNNGGHH!" said Walter, as he spat out some snow, but Dennis was already halfway down the street. He was going so fast that he didn't spot the Colonel. THUMP! They collided and flew into the air. Dennis landed on his skateboard and the Colonel landed on his toy soldiers.

"YOWEEE!" he hollered, leaping off the frozen soldier.

"You've interrupted parade, you young pipsqueak!"

"Oh, I reckon your soldiers deserve a day off in this cold weather!" Dennis exclaimed. He pulled out his peashooter and aimed it at the soldiers. "Time for the firing squad!"

POW! PING! ZIPP! The soldiers flew in all directions, landing headfirst in snowdrifts and disappearing into snowy gardens.

"STOP! HALT! DESERTERS!" blustered the Colonel , running this way and that, trying to catch his disappearing troops.

"Stand still, sir!"

"Exercise keeps you nimble!" Dennis chuckled, whizzing off down the street.

Curly was making ice sculptures in the front garden.

"What are they meant to be?" asked Dennis, critically.

"Monsters!" grinned Curly. "I've been making them every day. The softy across the street has been having nightmares!"

"Excellent menacing potential," Dennis grinned. "But I reckon we can do better than just a few monsters in your garden!"

Dennis whispered in Curly's ear, and a wide grin spread over Curly's face.

"Let's do it!" he chortled.

There was a flurry of ice, snow and carving. Dennis and Curly didn't even notice the storm getting worse and worse.

Soon, the gardens around Curly's house looked very different indeed. Ice goblins peered out of hedges. Ice vampires stood on window ledges. Ice dragons perched on water features.

"ARRRGGGHH!" screamed Mrs Hodges, when she opened her front door and came face to face with an ice troll. "EEEK!" squealed Bertie Blenkinsop, when he passed Curly's garden and saw an ice demon glaring at him. "Mumsy!" wailed the softy who lived across the road, when he saw the ice gargoyles peeping in at his bedroom window.

Dennis and Curly snorted with laughter as they heard the screams ringing out around them.

"What next?" asked Curly. "That was genius!"

66

Suddenly, all the streetlights made a fizzing sound and went out. Curly's mum opened the sitting room window.

"This is the last straw!" she bawled. "The electricity isn't working and the phone lines are down because of the storm! No heating, no TV and no way to escape!"

"Aha!" Dennis grinned, rubbing his hands together. "Beanotown is in my power!"

"Let's grab Pie Face and get menacing!" said Curly.

But when they turned to walk out of the garden, they were faced with a HUGE mound of snow. While they had been making their ice monsters, the storm had been busy. Everyone was snowed in!

"Nothing can stop the Menace!" Dennis declared. "Start digging, Curly! We've gotta rescue Pie Face!"

They dived into the snow and hollowed a tunnel out of the gate, up the street, across the road and through a hedge to Pie Face's front door.

"Oy! Pie Face!" yelled Dennis, hammering on the door. The snow had completely covered it, but Pie Face appeared on the other side of the cat flap. His eyes widened in amazement.

"You're just in time!" he gasped. "I've completely run out of pies! I'm getting pie-withdrawal rash!"

"Come on then!" said Dennis. "Let's go for supplies!"

"But I can't open the door!" Pie Face groaned.

Dennis thrust his hand through the cat flap and grabbed Pie Face by his collar.

"If you can't climb through a cat flap in an emergency pie situation, you're not worthy of the title 'menace'!" he stated. "Now squeeze through and let's go!"

In the end, Curly and Dennis had to pull with all their strength, but finally Pie Face shot through the cat flap with a loud POP! and landed in the snow tunnel.

"Awesome!" he grinned, looking around. "Can you dig one of these into town?"

"No worries," said Dennis. "But you need to tell us which way the bakery is."

"Easy!" said Pie Face, sniffing the air. "We can just follow my nose!"

"The only nose in Beanotown that can smell pies through seven-foot snowdrifts!" said Dennis proudly. "What a team!"

After ten minutes of tunnelling, they hit the door of the bakery.

"Never fails!" Pie Face grinned, tapping his nose.

"Hmm, but it looks like the shop's closed because of the snow," said Dennis. "Don't worry, I've got a plan!"

He pulled out his catapult and fired something at the lock. There was a creaking, cracking sound and the lock broke.

"Super-strength stink pellets!" he grinned. "Nothing can stand 'em!"

They pushed the door open and saw the baker, who was sitting behind his counter, munching fairy cakes sadly.

"Rescue!" he squealed, when he saw Dennis. "Oh, thank goodness! The locks froze and I've been stuck here for hours!"

"No problem, just follow the tunnel and you'll reach Pie Face's house," said Dennis.

"Thank you!" the baker cried, crawling into the tunnel. "Help yourself to all the food you want!"

The three menaces stared at each other as the baker disappeared down the tunnel.

"I reckon he might regret that," chuckled Pie Face, rubbing his belly.

They looked around the bakery. The shelves were lined with pies and cakes, muffins and pastries, biscuits and scones. Pie Face let out a long sigh of delight.

The sound of gobbling and swallowing filled the air, and the shelves emptied at top speed. Ten minutes later, the three menaces were sitting in the middle of the bakery, propping each other up and burping.

CHOMP!

"That was like my best dream ever," said Pie Face.

"Ooohh, my belly," Curly groaned.

"Come on, we haven't finished yet," said Dennis. "There's still loads of food out in the back room. Grab a bag each and fill it up – we're gonna need supplies!"

"For what?" asked Pie Face.

"For survival, dopey!" said Dennis. "Beanotown's run out of electricity, so we're gonna have to grab supplies and camp out!"

"In all this snow, we're gonna need a tent," said Curly.

"Where can we find a tent?" asked Pie Face groggily (he was still reeling from all those pies).

"Scout hut!" said Dennis and Curly at once.

They filled bags with as much food as they could carry, and then tunnelled across town to the scout hut. But when they reached the door, it was padlocked.

"I'm all outta stink pellets," said Dennis.

"Stumped!" groaned Curly. "What do we do now?"

"Nothing stops the Menace!" Dennis said, digging downwards again. He tunnelled under the hut and then pulled Mum's battery-operated egg whisk out of his back pocket.

"A whisk?" said Curly, scornfully.

"Excellent menacing equipment," Dennis told him. "Great for creating new hairstyles for soppy girls, tickling softies, and..." he turned the whisk on and sent it whirring through the wooden floorboards of the hut, "...drilling through floors!"

78

Soon they were inside the scout hut, rummaging for equipment.

"Be prepared!" grinned Dennis, slinging a tent onto his back and grabbing a frying pan. Curly and Pie Face piled blankets and pillows into their arms. Just then, there was a whimper from the corner. Dennis flung some grappling hooks and ropes out of the way, and found the scoutmaster whimpering and sucking his thumb.

"I'm s-s-scared of s-s-storms and s-s-snow!" he burbled.

"You're a s-s-softy," Dennis chortled. "Here, have a pie and go down that tunnel to Pie Face's house. His mum'll make you a nice cup of tea."

"Oh thank you!" gasped the scoutmaster, hurrying down the tunnel.

"Okay," said Curly. "We've got tents, we've got pies, we've got a frying pan... what else do we need?"

"SAUSAGES!" yelled Dennis and Pie Face.

They dived back into the tunnel and cut their way through the snow to the butcher's shop. The door was open and the whole shop was filled with snow. Dennis leapt out of the tunnel.

"Can I help you?" said a muffled voice.

Dennis leaned over the counter and dug snow out of the way until he spotted the top of the butcher's head.

"What are you doing there?" asked Dennis.

"I had the door open when the storm blew up," said the butcher mournfully. "Before I could move, the whole shop had turned into a snowdrift."

"We'll soon have you outta there," said Dennis.

He pulled a small paper bag from his pocket and offered it to Curly and Pie Face.

"Yum, gobstoppers!" Pie Face cried, popping two into his mouth.

"My favourite!" said Curly, taking three.

Dennis sniggered.

"Extra-fiery devilishly hot gobstoppers!" he whispered.

"ARRGGHHH!" yelled Pie Face and Curly at the same time. Their fiery breath melted the snow around the butcher!

"HAH!" Dennis grinned. "I knew it'd work!"

As Pie Face and Curly cooled down by popping snow into their mouths, the butcher wrung Dennis by the hand.

"Help yourself to whatever you want from the shop!" he said. And Gnasher can have free sausages whenever he wants them!"

"Thanks! Just head back down the tunnel to Pie Face's house," said Dennis.

While Curly and Pie Face were balancing ice cubes on their tongues, Dennis filled a bag with sausages, burgers and prime steaks.

"Come on, you wimps," he said. "We've got a survival shelter to build!"

They tunnelled out of town to the park, and found a clearing.

"Right," said Dennis, "Pie Face, you get the tents up while Curly and I do the food."

Soon they had three lopsided tents and a campfire built high, with

sausages and burgers ready to cook over the flames.

"We've thought of everything!" grinned Pie Face, as his stomach rumbled.

"Not quite, dear!" said a voice. "You forgot about matches!"

A huge crowd of people was coming out of the tunnel, led by Pie Face's mum!

"And you forgot drinks too!" she said, pointing behind her. The scoutmaster and the baker were carrying a huge crate of fizzy pop!

"What are you all doing here?" gasped Pie Face, gaping as the clearing filled up with softies, parents and everyone Dennis had menaced for years.

"Catapults at the ready!" said Dennis, catching sight of Sergeant Slipper, who was lighting the campfire.

"No," said Pie Face's mum. "We need your help. Now all the power is down, this is the only place in Beanotown with heat, light and food!"

"Eh?" said Dennis.

"You're a hero!" said his dad, coming and patting him on the back.

"Am I dreaming?" asked Curly. "I think that gobstopper's fried my brain!"

"Three cheers for Dennis!" cried the Colonel, grabbing a burger.

Dennis chortled in disbelief as everyone cheered.

"I reckon we've taught Beanotown an important lesson!" he said. "Menacing is the greatest survival skill of all!"

More Bumper  fun...

1–84539–202–7

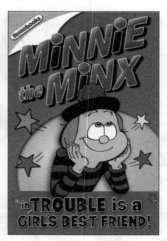

1–84539–203–5

1–84539–095–4

1–84539–096–2

... make sure you've got them all!

1–84539–097–0

1–84539–098–9

1–84539–204–8

1–84539–205–1

Written by RACHEL ELLIOT

Illustrated by BARRIE APPLEBY

published under licence by

meadowside
CHILDREN'S BOOKS
185 Fleet Street, London, EC4A 2HS

10 9 8 7 6 5 4 3 2